Published in the United States of America by Crown Publishers, Inc.,
225 Park Avenue South, New York, New York 10003
Published in Great Britain by Walker Books, Ltd.,
184-192 Drummond Street, London NW1 3HP
CROWN, IT'S GREAT TO READ!, and logo are trademarks of Crown Publishers, Inc.
Manufactured in Italy.
Library of Congress Cataloging-in-Publication Data
Baynton, Martin.
Fifty and the great race.
Summary: Fifty the tractor must win the race at the
annual fair or risk being scrapped for junk.
[1. Tractors—Fiction. 2. Racing—Fiction. 3. Fairs
—Fiction] I. Title.
PZ7.B347Fgf 1986 [E] 86-8811
ISBN 0-517-56354-1
10 9 8 7 6 5 4 3 2 1   First American Edition

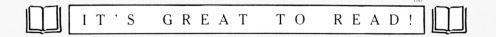

IT'S GREAT TO READ! ™

FIFTY
AND THE
GREAT RACE

Martin Baynton

CROWN PUBLISHERS, INC., NEW YORK

It was the morning of the County
Fair and the farmer's van had broken
down.

"We'll have to go on the tractor," he
grumbled to Wally.

Fifty the tractor was delighted.

Fifty had never been to a fair before and he felt very excited. His friend Norris the rat was not so pleased.

Norris peered out of Fifty's toolbox and sniffed the air. He could smell trouble.

The man at the gate laughed as
Wally drove Fifty through.

"What did you bring him for?" the
man said, chuckling. "The Old
Machinery Exhibition?"
The farmer was furious.

They drove past a man selling new tractors. He pointed at Fifty.

"Scrap him!" he shouted. "Buy a new one!"

"Perhaps I will," said the farmer.

Wally was horrified. "You can't scrap Fifty. He's the best tractor in the world!"

"Prove it," growled the farmer.

"There's a tractor race today. You enter
Fifty. If he loses, I'll scrap him."

That afternoon Fifty lined up with
the other tractors. Next to him stood
Big Blue, a powerful new tractor driven
by the salesman.

"Ready, set, GO!" cried the starter.
And with a great churning of grass
and dirt the tractors roared away.

Fifty shot off the line and raced
ahead of the others.

Norris opened the toolbox.
"Trouble?" he asked.

"Big, big trouble." Fifty panted.

Fifty reached the halfway mark first.
Here the drivers had to stop and load
up with heavy sacks of grain.

Wally was fast, but the salesman was faster. He could lift two sacks at a time! Wally couldn't believe it.

Big Blue was soon loaded. He laughed at Fifty, opened his throttle, and raced toward the finish line. No one noticed his extra passenger.

Wally loaded his last sack and scrambled into his seat. Fifty tore away in hot pursuit. It was now or never. He had to win.

Fifty strained every nut and bolt in his effort to catch up. He pushed himself until his water began to boil. But it was hopeless! He was beaten.

Wally closed his eyes. He had done his best but it wasn't good enough. Fifty was sure to be scrapped.

Then one of the sacks on Big Blue burst open. It was full of chicken feathers!

"Big Blue cheated!" cried the judge. "Fifty wins!"

"You did it!" said Norris, climbing into the toolbox.

Then Fifty saw that Norris was covered in feathers.

"No," Fifty said. "*We* did it!"